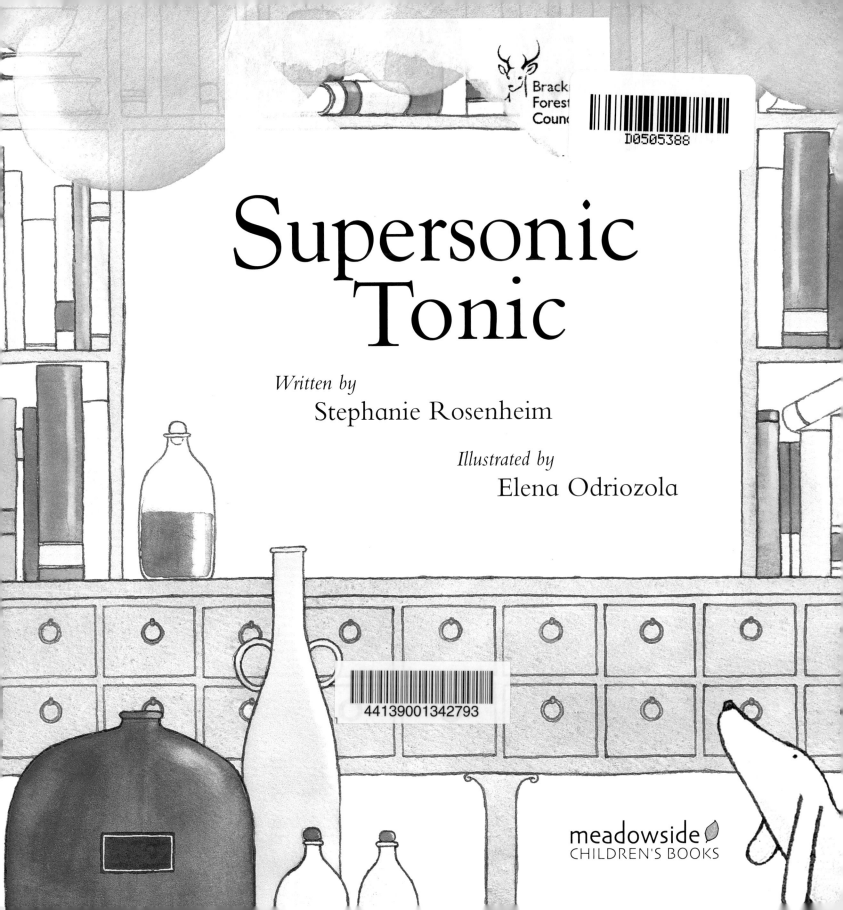

Supersonic Tonic

Written by
Stephanie Rosenheim

Illustrated by
Elena Odriozola

meadowside
CHILDREN'S BOOKS

Madeleine Daisy,

the smallest of five,
thought Grandpa terrific,
and really alive.
But Grandpa grew old
and he took to his bed,

Madeleine Daisy saw
trouble ahead…

He lay there with blanket
on wobbly knee,

crinkly…
wrinkly…
aged 93.

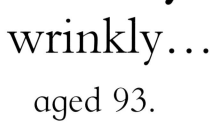

"The doctor just says…

I₁
SHOULD₂ **KEEP**₃
OUT OF TROUBLE.₄
THE THINGS₅
THAT HE GAVE ME₆

Just made me
see double.

"I think I should stay here,
and dream of the past,
coping…
        …and hoping
I feel better fast."

Now Madeleine Daisy
had read in a book
of a brilliant brew you
could learn how to cook.

She read, *"if you take this particular tonic,*
you'll fly like a flash!
You'll feel
supersonic!"

So Madeleine Daisy
went into her room,
and made up this potion
for him to consume.

Then she kissed all his wrinkles,
she gave him a smile,
and told him he needed
to rest for a while.

She gave him the tonic
and told him 'goodnight'…

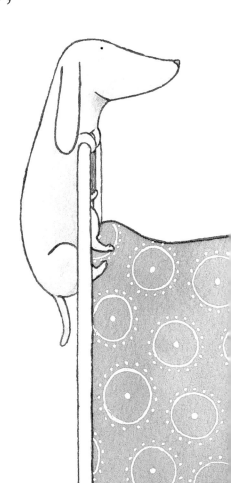

…kissed him,

hugged him…

…and turned out the light.

When Madeleine Daisy
awoke before dawn,
she saw someone bounding
across the front lawn.

She leapt out of bed,
grabbed her favourite hat,
and was out of the door
in ten seconds flat.

What was it....?

Who was it....?

Where had he gone…?

Oh Grandpa! No! Grandpa!
Oh, what had she done?!

Now Grandpa was running,
faster and faster…
and when she ran to him,
he sprinted right past her!

He jumped over bushes,
and ran to the edge,

then bolted,

and
vaulted,

the
neighbouring
hedge.

Madeleine's eyes grew
wide with surprise.
She looked at the muscles
that bulged in his thighs.

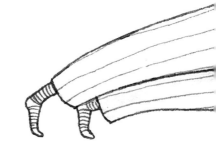

Then Madeleine knew
she was on to a winner…
a spoonful of tonic
before every dinner!

Doing the limbo under
the door…

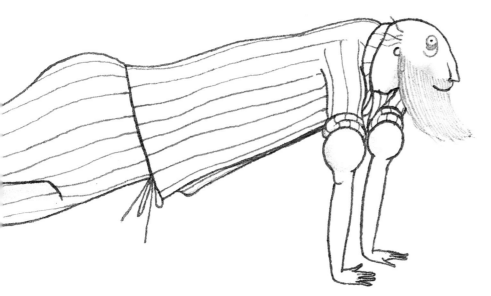

press ups...

sit ups...

cartwheels galore.

As daylight was breaking,
the neighbourhood stirred,
with soft sounds of creatures,
both feathered and furred.

Happy, together,
they watched the sun climb…

…but Grandpa was restless,
back in his prime…

So he hurtled off over
the rooftops instead,

whilst Madeleine…

tired…

...crawled back into bed.

For my Dad,
with love.
S.R.

For Isabel and Cristina.
E.O.

First published in 2005
by Meadowside Children's Books,
185 Fleet Street, London, EC4A 2HS.

Text © Stephanie Rosenheim 2005
Illustrations © Elena Odriozola 2005

The rights of Stephanie Rosenheim and
Elena Odriozola to be identified as the
author and illustrator of this work have been
asserted by them in accordance with the Copyright,
Designs and Patents Act, 1988.

A CIP catalogue record for this book
is available from the British Library.
Printed in U.A.E.

10 9 8 7 6 5 4 3 2 1